THIS BEAR, THAT BEAR!

A TEMPLAR BOOK

First published in the UK in 2017 by Templar Publishing,
part of the Bonnier Publishing Group,
The Plaza, 535 King's Road, London, SW10 0SZ
www.templarco.co.uk
www.bonnierpublishing.com

1 3 5 7 9 10 8 6 4 2

ISBN 978-1-78370-628-0

Designed by Olivia Cook
Edited by Katie Haworth
Printed in China

THIS BEAR, THAT BEAR!

Sian Wheatcroft

t

templar publishing

Come on, Little Bear,
there's a bear parade today.
Who do you think we'll see?
Come with me – this way!

Look it's . . .

likes-to-wear-a-hat bear.

Brown bear,

clown bear,

about-to-fall-down bear.

Tall bear,

small bear,

loves-to-kick-a-ball bear.

GOAL!

Cheeky bear,

sneaky bear,

fabulously geeky bear.

Funny bear,

rumbly-in-his-tummy bear.

mummy bear,

Ready bear,

steady bear,

I-really-love-my-teddy bear.

Gold bear,

old bear,

very, very cold bear.

ICE BEAR

Hairy bear,

fairy bear,

WHOOOOOO!

really-far-too-scary bear.

Dude bear,

rude bear,

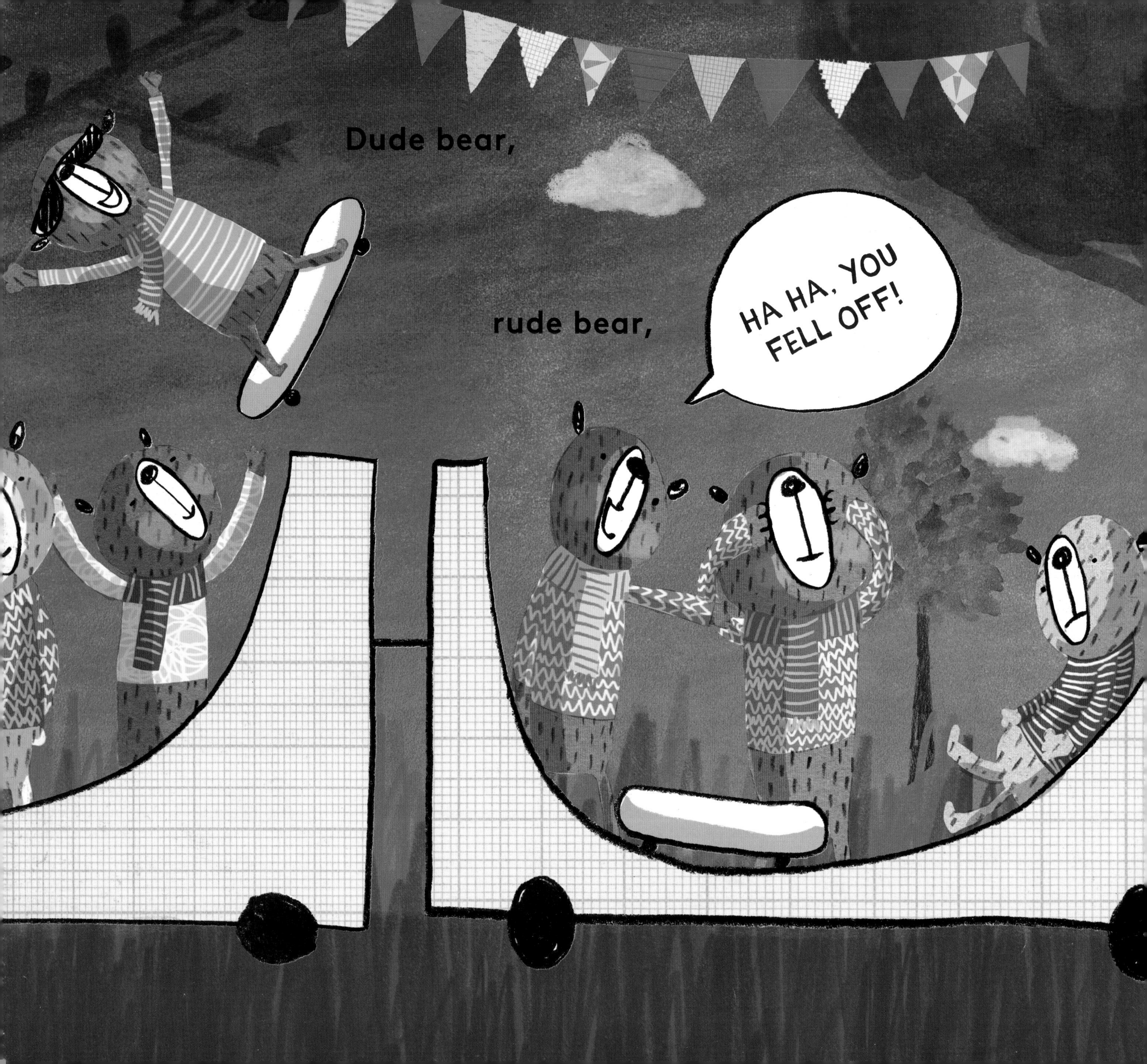

in-a-bad-mood bear.

FANCY DRESS CONTEST

Proud bear,

big-fluffy-cloud bear.

loud bear,

Friend bear,

trend bear,

nearly-at-the-end bear.

Light bear . . .

. . . night bear . . .

. . . tucked-up-tight bear.

More picture books from Templar:

ISBN: 978-1-78370-381-4 (hardback)
978-1-78370-574-0 (paperback)

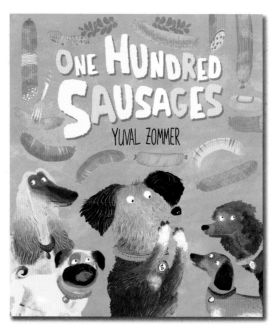

ISBN: 978-1-78370-575-7 (hardback)
978-1-78370-576-4 (paperback)

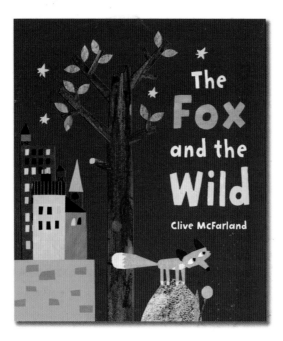

ISBN: 978-1-78370-386-9 (hardback)
978-1-78370-387-6 (paperback)

ISBN: 978-1-78370-238-1 (hardback)
978-1-78370-239-8 (paperback)